DRUGS
HEROIN
A MyReportLinks.com Book

Aileen Weintraub

MyReportLinks.com Books
an imprint of

Enslow Publishers, Inc.
Box 398, 40 Industrial Road
Berkeley Heights, NJ 07922
USA

MyReportLinks.com Books

MyReportLinks.com Books, an imprint of Enslow Publishers, Inc. MyReportLinks® is a registered trademark of Enslow Publishers, Inc.

Copyright © 2005 by Enslow Publishers, Inc.

All rights reserved.

No part of this book may be reproduced by any means without the written permission of the publisher.

Library of Congress Cataloging-in-Publication Data

Weintraub, Aileen, 1973–
  Heroin / Aileen Weintraub.
    p. cm. — (Drugs)
  Includes bibliographical references and index.
  ISBN 0-7660-5275-3
  1. Heroin—History—Juvenile literature. 2. Heroin habit—Juvenile literature. I. Title. II. Drugs (Berkeley Heights, N.J.)
  RC568.H4W45 2005
  362.29'3—dc22
                          2004007581

Printed in the United States of America

10 9 8 7 6 5 4 3 2 1

To Our Readers:
Through the purchase of this book, you and your library gain access to the Report Links that specifically back up this book.
The Publisher will provide access to the Report Links that back up this book and will keep these Report Links up to date on **www.myreportlinks.com** for five years from the book's first publication date.
We have done our best to make sure all Internet addresses in this book were active and appropriate when we went to press. However, the author and the Publisher have no control over, and assume no liability for, the material available on those Internet sites or on other Web sites they may link to.
The usage of the MyReportLinks.com Books Web site is subject to the terms and conditions stated on the Usage Policy Statement on **www.myreportlinks.com**.
A password may be required to access the Report Links that back up this book. The password is found on the bottom of page 4 of this book.
Any comments or suggestions can be sent by e-mail to comments@myreportlinks.com or to the address on the back cover.

Photo Credits: AP/Wide World Photos, p. 11; Central Intelligence Agency, p. 12; © 1998 PBS and WGBH/Frontline, p. 33; © 1999–2004 Narcotics Anonymous, p. 40; © 2002 Narconon International, p. 28; © 2004 The Mentor Foundation International, p. 41; Digital Stock Photos: Government and Social Issues, p. 23; Library of Congress, p. 19; MyReportLinks.com Books, p. 4; National Archives, p. 38; National Institute on Drug Abuse/U.S. Department of Health and Human Services, p. 26; Office of National Drug Control Policy, pp. 16, 21, 31; Stockbyte: Sensitive Issues, pp. 1, 14, 15, 30, 35, 36, 42; U.S. Drug Enforcement Administration, pp. 1, 3, 9, 18.

Cover Photo: Stockbyte: Sensitive Issues (needle and spoon); U.S. Drug Enforcement Administration (powder).

Disclaimer: While the stories of abuse in this book are real, many of the names have been changed.

MyReportLinks.com Books

Report Links	4
Heroin Facts	9
1 Wasted Talent	10
2 The History of Heroin	16
3 Effects of Heroin	26
4 How Heroin is Produced and Sold	33
5 Recovery	38
Glossary	45
Chapter Notes	46
Further Reading	47
Index	48

About MyReportLinks.com Books

MyReportLinks.com Books
Great Books, Great Links, Great for Research!

The Internet sites listed on the next four pages can save you hours of research time. These Internet sites—we call them "Report Links"—are constantly changing, but we keep them up to date on our Web site.

Give it a try! Type http://www.myreportlinks.com into your browser, click on the series title, then the book title, and scroll down to the Report Links listed for this book.

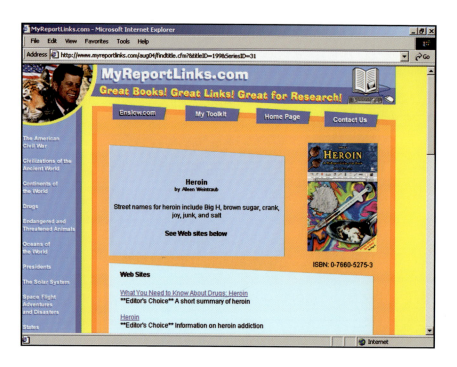

The Report Links will bring you to great source documents, photographs, and illustrations. MyReportLinks.com Books save you time, feature Report Links that are kept up to date, and make report writing easier than ever!

Please see "To Our Readers" on the copyright page for important information about this book, the MyReportLinks.com Web site, and the Report Links that back up this book.

Please enter **DRH1895** if asked for a password.

MyReportLinks.com Books

Tools   Search   Notes   Discuss   Go!

Report Links

The Internet sites described below can be accessed at
http://www.myreportlinks.com

▶**What You Need to Know About Drugs: Heroin** *Editor's choice
This fact sheet explains what heroin is and what it looks like. It also provides information on how heroin is used and what it does to the body.

▶**Heroin** *Editor's choice
This Web site provides information on the background, effects, prevalence of use, and availability of heroin. The consequences of using heroin, and facts about treatment programs are included.

▶**From Flowers to Heroin** *Editor's choice
Learn how farmers in different parts of the world grow poppies. Opium gum is harvested from the poppy flowers and dried. It is then sent to refineries and processed into morphine and heroin in a multi-stage procedure using chemicals and additives.

▶**Drug Trends: Heroin** *Editor's choice
HIV/AIDS, hepatitis, and other infections are more common among heroin users who share needles. Tolerance levels, symptoms of withdrawal, and the factors involved in a heroin overdose are also discussed.

▶**The Opium Kings** *Editor's choice
PBS chronicles thirty years of Burma's heroin trade, as well as the rise and fall of warlord Khun Sa. Learn more about the history, manufacturing, trafficking, and effects of heroin. Charts, maps, and interviews are also included.

▶**Mind Over Matters: Opiates** *Editor's choice
Opiates, such as heroin, effect the brain and make it difficult for brain cells to function once dependency occurs. Learn more about opiates, the nervous system, and the brain at this Web site.

Any comments? Contact us: comments@myreportlinks.com   5

Report Links

The Internet sites described below can be accessed at http://www.myreportlinks.com

▶ American Association for the Treatment of Opioid Dependence
The American Association for the Treatment of Opioid Dependence (AATOD) supports and promotes methadone use in the treatment of opiate addicts. One of its goals is to make sure that abusers have access to good quality, safe, and ethical medical care.

▶ Basic Facts About Drugs: Heroin
The American Council for Drug Education explains the short- and long-term effects of heroin and why it is so dangerous to your health. Slang names are noted.

▶ Drugs: What You Should Know
This fact sheet explains what heroin is and what it looks like. It also provides information on how heroin is used, its street names, and the dangers of using such an addictive drug.

▶ Drugs and Alcohol: Straight Talk
Written for young women and girls, this article provides an overview of drugs and why they are dangerous.

▶ Heroin
This article explores the history of opiates. Topics covered include how users ingest heroin, as well as its effects on the brain and other organs.

▶ Heroin: Drug Facts
This Web site provides information on the extent of heroin use, its health effects, and treatment options for addicts. Statistics for heroin-related arrests, production and trafficking, and street names are also included.

▶ Heroin: StreetDrugs.org
Read this overview of heroin and opium, including information on user statistics, history, and street names. Pictures of the poppy plant are included along with physical descriptions of heroin and opium.

▶ Heroin: Wichita
According to this Web site from the Wichita, Kansas, police department, India is one of the largest suppliers of raw opium in the world. Learn more about how heroin is manufactured and some of the many health risks associated with using the drug.

Any comments? Contact us: **comments@myreportlinks.com**

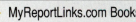

Tools   Search   Notes   Discuss

Report Links

The Internet sites described below can be accessed at http://www.myreportlinks.com

▶ **Heroin Addiction**
Learn about the effects and symptoms of heroin use and the overwhelming depression experienced by people who take the drug. Withdrawal and treatment programs are also covered.

▶ **History of Heroin**
Heroin has a long history in the United States. Originally invented in Germany by Bayer, the drug was marketed in America as a safe alternative to morphine and opium. Learn more about how and why heroin became illegal.

▶ **The Mentor Foundation**
The Mentor Foundation seeks to promote the well-being and health of young people around the world. This organization offers information, support, and effective strategies that will prevent children and teens from using drugs.

▶ **Methadone**
Methadone is a safe and legal medication used in the treatment of heroin addiction. Learn more about how this drug reduces the cravings associated with heroin use and how it minimizes withdrawal symptoms.

▶ **NAADAC, The Association for Addiction Professionals**
NAADAC strives to create healthier families and communities through drug prevention, intervention, and quality treatment. Read about the efforts of this organization.

▶ **Narcotics Anonymous**
Narcotics Anonymous (NA) is an organization for recovering drug addicts. The NA's Twelve-Step Program can be found in over one hundred countries. Follow the links to find worldwide contact and meeting information. Bulletins, reports, and periodicals are also available.

▶ **New Approaches Seek To Expand Naltrexone Use in Heroin Treatment**
Learn about Naltrexone, a drug used in one of the newer treatment programs for opiate addiction, at this Web site. It works by blocking the addict from being able to get high, but the patient still goes through withdrawal.

▶ **NIDA InfoFacts: Heroin**
Read about the health hazards of using heroin, including the risks of infectious diseases such as HIV/AIDS and hepatitis. Learn more about heroin withdrawal and treatment programs.

Any comments? Contact us: comments@myreportlinks.com

Report Links

The Internet sites described below can be accessed at http://www.myreportlinks.com

▶ Opiates
Opiates, including opium, morphine, and heroin, have been used for years as pain relievers. How do they work, and what do they do to your brain? Learn more about opiates, and try a crossword puzzle to test your knowledge.

▶ Opium Poppy Cultivation and Heroin Processing in Southeast Asia
The Golden Triangle Area of mainland Southeast Asia is known for its cultivation of the opium poppy, an important cash crop for farmers in the area. Learn more about the poppy plant and how it is used to make heroin.

▶ Partnership for a Drug-Free America
Partnership for a Drug-Free America focuses its efforts on reducing substance abuse in America. At this organization's Web site you will find a recent study on teen drug use, an e-newsletter you can sign up for, and stories about real people.

▶ Pulse Check: Trends in Drug Abuse
This Web site provides information on heroin abusers and markets. It also describes changes in use, treatment programs, drug-related criminal activity, and distribution patterns for heroin in the United States.

▶ Street Terms: Drugs and the Drug Trade, Drug Type: Heroin
Learn the terms used by drug dealers and users to describe heroin and the activities surrounding its use.

▶ Tips for Teens: The Truth About Heroin
This Web site clears up some of the myths concerning heroin and helps to give a clear picture of the effects, signs, and risks involved in using the drug. Learn more about heroin addiction.

▶ What Are the Treatments for Heroin Addiction?
You will learn about a variety of effective treatments (including methadone programs) for heroin addiction at this Web site. Treatment is often much more effective when the abuse is identified early.

▶ What's Up with Heroin?
Learn what heroin looks like and where it comes from. You will find information on how the drug is made and used, its nicknames, and the mental and physical effects it has on people.

8   Any comments? Contact us: **comments@myreportlinks.com**

HEROIN FACTS

- Approximately 3.1 million Americans have tried heroin at least once.

- In the year 2000, 13.3 metric tons of heroin were consumed.

- Heroin users spent a combined total of $10 billion on their drug habit in the year 2000.

- In 2002, 1.6 percent of eighth graders and 1.7 percent of twelfth graders reported using heroin at least once.

- The four main areas of heroin production are Mexico, South America, Southeast Asia, and Southwest Asia.

- Street level heroin usually sells for ten dollars a dose.

- According to the FBI, heroin accounted for 9.7 percent of drug arrests for sale and manufacturing and 23.1 percent for sales in 2001.

- In fiscal year 2001, federal heroin offenders received an average sentence of 63.4 months in prison.

- In 2003, there were 93,519 visits to emergency rooms involving the use of heroin.

- During fiscal year 2002, United States federal agencies seized 6,900 pounds of heroin.

- Those admitted for heroin treatment in 2002 were mostly male (68.5 percent) and caucasian (47.7 percent). The average age was thirty-six years old.

Chapter 1

Janis Joplin was a teenager growing up in Port Arthur, Texas, in the 1950s. She was a very smart girl who did not really fit in with the crowd. Many considered Joplin an outcast because of her strange clothing choices and the fact that she did not look like all the other girls. She was different. She began to rebel by spending time with a group of adventurous boys. It was during this time in her life that Janis began to discover her talent for singing.

Her voice was so amazing and original that she would soon become one of the most famous rock stars of all time. During the early years of her career, Joplin mostly sang in coffee shops. It was the early 1960s, and rock and roll was just beginning to become popular.

Even with her singing career off to a start, Joplin suffered from depression. She was not always well liked, and she never felt good about herself. The singer never felt quite as pretty as the other girls. She had low self-esteem.

Joplin moved to California looking for excitement. In the 1960s, California was buzzing with people searching for new experiences. Many young people known as hippies chose to leave home. Often they ended up camping in parks, wandering from place to place, and living on the streets. This often meant that they were an easy target for people who wanted to take advantage of them. Drugs and alcohol became a big problem.

Janis Joplin began drinking a lot of alcohol. As she became more involved in the rock scene, she started doing drugs, too. At first, she did amphetamines, also called speed. She quickly became addicted. Her weight dropped to eighty-eight pounds, and she was

> Wasted Talent

▲ Janis Joplin is shown here in 1968 performing with the band Big Brother and the Holding Company.

MyReportLinks.com Books

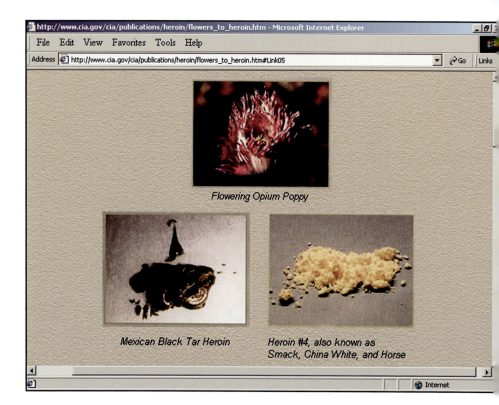

▲ Raw opium gum from an opium poppy plant can be used to make two forms of heroin commonly found in the United States, Mexican black tar heroin (left) and heroin #4 (right).

always nervous. Eventually her addiction became so bad that she could no longer do everyday tasks. She could not even make a simple decision on her own. With help, Joplin went back to her hometown and tried to clean up her life. She managed to stop using speed by seeing a therapist, changing her lifestyle and the people she hung around with, and eating better.

Joplin was now able to concentrate on her career once again. In 1966, she moved back to California and joined a band called Big Brother and the Holding Company. She concentrated on a style of music known as the blues. Her lyrics were about the hardships of life. At this time, over fifteen hundred new bands began to pop up in San Francisco. Joplin's voice made the band stand out above the rest. Her career was about to take off. She began to dress more outrageously than ever before. She was creating an image for herself. Though the singer had intended to stay off drugs, everyone around her seemed to be using them. Wherever she went, people were partying and drinking. The temptation was too much for Joplin, and she was not able to resist.

As Joplin became more of a superstar, she did more and more drugs. Fame and fortune came very fast for her. She was living out her dream. People actually became violent trying to get tickets to see her perform. Even though it seems as though she had everything she could want, she was unhappy. Like many others who rise quickly to fame, Joplin could not handle all the publicity. Her behavior continued to become wilder. She got into fights and would curse on stage.

As a famous star, Joplin was under constant pressure. She had a very busy schedule, and she did not always know whom to trust. She often felt that people were using her because of her star status. The singer began to think that the only way she could find happiness was through drugs. She started to use heroin in search of feeling something other than sadness. In reality, the heroin only numbed her pain so she felt nothing. Even surrounded by all her fans, new friends, and band members, Joplin was incredibly lonely. When a concert did not go as she planned or if she got a bad review, the first thing she did was reach for more heroin.[1]

Joplin's drug habit continued to get worse. If anyone tried to help her, she would become very angry. She was destroying herself. The singer made a few halfhearted attempts to kick her drug habit, but nothing seemed to help.

Even through her drug use, Joplin's career managed to reach amazing heights. She moved from one band to the next, making more money than she could have ever dreamed. She continued to host wild parties with a lot of drugs and drinking. Soon, this lifestyle and the effects of the drugs took its toll.

Joplin played at the famous Woodstock Festival of 1969. Her performance was only average. She was becoming ill-tempered and selfish. Her voice and her energy onstage were suffering. Joplin was completely miserable, and it showed. As her addiction got worse, so did her personality. No one wanted to be around her. She was always angry or stressed out. Joplin even overdosed on heroin as many as five times but somehow managed to stay alive.[2] Even when she tried to stop doing heroin, the singer would continue to drink large amounts of alcohol. Then Joplin would go back to using heroin. In the meantime, she saw friends of hers, including other rock stars, die of heroin overdoses. This bothered her, but it was not enough to make her stop.

In October 1970, despite all the drug use, Joplin's career was going very well. She decided to give up some of her wild ways and settle down. She was even planning to get married. She had also

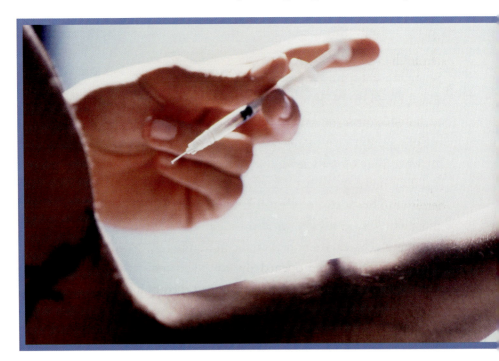

▲ Janis Joplin started using a variety of drugs after moving to San Francisco. Heroin, however, was the deadliest. Most users inject heroin, although it can be smoked or snorted.

Intravenous users melt heroin into a liquid form before injecting it into their veins. More than one addict has died with a needle in their arm as a result.

planned to sing and tour for only two more years. By then she would have saved enough money to retire for the rest of her life if she wanted to.

Yet, she could not stop using. On Saturday, October 3, Joplin called her dealer for some more heroin. She used less heroin than usual because she had a recording session later that day at the studio. She knew she would need to be able to function. After the recording session, with heroin still in her system, she went to a local bar with some of her friends. At about 12:30 A.M. on October 4, Joplin went back to her hotel room. She injected some more heroin into her body and then left her room to buy cigarettes. She spoke with the desk clerk for a while and asked for change for the cigarette machine. After she bought her cigarettes, Joplin headed back to her room. She opened the door and took two steps in. Then, she fell down dead. Janis Joplin had died of a heroin overdose in the prime of her career at the age of twenty-seven.

Chapter 2

The History of Heroin

Smack, H, skag, junk, dope, skin popping, horse, jive, shag. These are all street names for heroin. Heroin is a highly addictive drug that comes from the opium poppy plant. The opium poppy is grown in the Middle East, Southeast Asia, Mexico, and parts of Central and South America. Opium is the raw drug that comes from the sap of the poppy plant. Drugs that come from opium

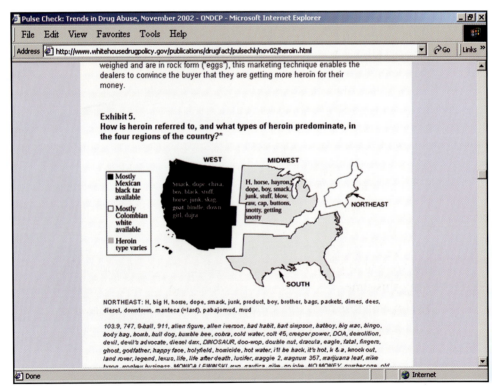

▲ This chart shows the most common forms of heroin found in each region of the United States, as well as the most common street names for each type.

are called opiates. It is not until the opium has been chemically altered in a laboratory that it becomes heroin.

Other drugs that are made from the opium poppy are codeine (used to stop coughing) and morphine (a painkiller). While opium does have these medical benefits, it is also highly addictive. A side effect of opium is that people can begin to have very unpleasant thoughts and dreams. Opium addicts tend to appear as if they no longer care about anything, and they begin to neglect their health and their families.

Opium use goes back to ancient times. Five thousand years ago, the Sumerians called it "the joy plant." Three thousand years ago, the ancient Egyptians recorded their use of opium as both a cure-all drug and a poison. By the year 800 A.D., opium was being brought to China. Within the next eight hundred years, opium became very popular in Asia. First, it was chiefly used as a medicine; then the British sold it in China as a recreational drug. More and more people in China began using the drug. Many lives were ruined because of opium use. In record numbers, people became addicted. In 1729, the Chinese finally made opium use illegal. This hardly got rid of the drug problem.

The Opium War

By 1838, even though opium was illegal in China, many people still used it. Opium dens became a popular place for people to go to use the drug in secrecy. These dens were dark and hidden away so people could sneak in without being caught. It is thought that there were about 2 million people addicted to opium in China during this time.

The emperor of China called upon Lin Zexu, a governor of the Chinese province Hu Huang. He was given the job of wiping out the opium problem. He started by arresting anyone who sold the drug.

The next step was to open up a clinic for people who wanted help getting off the drug. Lin opened his first clinic in the city of

Canton, a port city where there was a lot of opium use. This is mainly because British ships were smuggling opium into China through Canton.

Lin knew that to make the drug problem go away he would have to stop the British from bringing the opium to China. This was not easy because opium was big business for the British. The British did not take Lin's concerns seriously. Corrupt Chinese officials allowed British ships to pass through with opium, as long as the British were willing to pay a price.

Lin was forced to take extreme measures. He decided to stop trading with all Western merchants. Even this did not stop opium from coming into China. The British started docking their ships

▲ *Heroin is made from opium, a substance that comes from the sap of the poppy plant. This is what opium poppies look like.*

▲ This painting, called The War in China, *depicts an attack on the Canton River during the Opium Wars. China fought against Great Britain to end the opium trade, but the British were victorious.*

at other ports with less security. The situation kept getting worse. The British were angry that they were losing money on the opium trade. They sent warships to frighten the Chinese into allowing trade to continue. Lin had his own warships and sent those out in return. The battle had begun. The Chinese were no match for the British ships. The British won an easy victory. This was only one battle of many that would take place between the British and the Chinese over opium. The Chinese were never able to defeat British forces, and the Opium War officially ended in 1842.

▶ Opium in the United States

While the Opium War raged on, people in the United States were beginning to use the drug more often. In the beginning, opium was seen as a wonder drug that could cure many illnesses. By the

1850s, however, opium use was a big problem in the United States. Opium contains morphine, codeine, and thebaine. Morphine was isolated from opium and is the most powerful of the three chemicals. It was thought that morphine would not be addictive. This turned out to be a big mistake.

The Invention of a New Drug

In 1874, a London scientist named C. R. Alder Wright was looking for a drug that would be less addictive than morphine. This was the beginning phase of the invention of heroin. In 1898, Heinrich Dreser, a scientist working for the Bayer pharmaceutical company of Germany, produced heroin as a drug to treat illnesses such as tuberculosis, bronchitis, and asthma. Heroin was also an ingredient in many cough medicines. Besides being a cure-all for sickness, it was supposed to help people stop their morphine addiction.

People were taking heroin without even knowing it. Before 1906, there were no laws in the United States that said companies had to list their ingredients on their products. The Pure Food and Drug Act of 1906 forced manufacturers to put ingredients on their product labels so people could know what they were eating or taking.

It turned out that heroin was even more addictive than morphine. People were becoming addicted to heroin in record numbers.

Heroin Use Spreads

Smoking opium was very fashionable in the early 1900s. The United States government started cracking down on its use. Users started turning to heroin because it was cheaper than opium and easier to hide. After 1910, heroin use in the United States spread quickly. During this time, heroin was often called "junk." This was because people were so desperate for heroin that they would look through dumpsters for valuables. If they could sell something, they could make enough money to buy heroin.

The History of Heroin

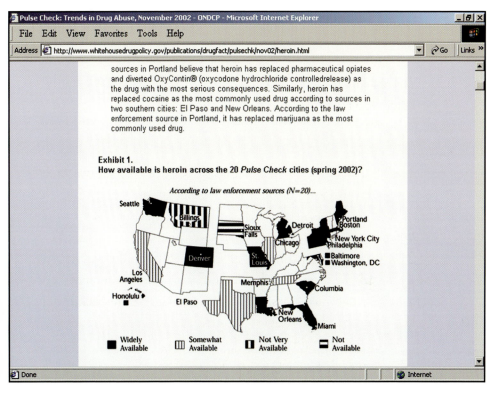

▲ In 2002, an organization called Pulse Check did a study to see how easy it was to obtain heroin in certain cities. Alarmingly, in twelve of the twenty cities it was widely available.

In the twentieth century, the Chinese, who previously tried to stop opium from coming into their own country, now became the main suppliers of opiates to the United States. Many heroin addicts were teenagers, and some were part of street gangs. Sometimes gangs made their members use heroin before they could become part of the group. In 1919, forty-four clinics opened that actually supplied addicts with heroin in hopes of helping them. The clinics registered the addicts and tried to collect information. They hoped that this process would eventually help abusers get off drugs. Addicts knew that they could get heroin on the street without being registered. The clinics failed. They were soon made illegal and shut down.

The U.S. Congress responded to the heroin problem in America. The Heroin Act of 1924 made it completely illegal for anyone to manufacture, possess, or use the drug for any purpose.

By the mid-twentieth century, New York City was known as the heroin capital of the United States. Ninety percent of all known addicts lived within 180 miles of Manhattan. Poor people began to use heroin to forget their problems. However, it did not stay a poor person's drug for very long. By 1965, heroin spread to the middle class. People began using heroin on street corners and on college campuses.

The Drug Culture

In 1957, a writer named Jack Kerouac published a book titled *On the Road*. His book became the gospel for a new group of young people called the Beat Generation. The heroes of this book traveled across the country looking for adventure. The Beats, as this generation of youths came to be known, wished to follow this example. Kerouac was heavily into drugs and so were his friends. They wrote about drugs in their books. One of Kerouac's friends, an author named William Burroughs, was heavily into heroin and even wrote a book called *Junky*.

These writers had a lot of influence on the young people of the time. They paved the way for an accepted drug culture in the United States.[1] The 1960s began a new kind of freedom with a lot of drug use and experimentation. Crime and drug abuse were on the rise. It cut across all boundaries, including race, age, and class. Between 1960 and 1970, heroin use rose from about fifty thousand to five hundred thousand people.

Celebrities and Heroin

Today, heroin use is not limited to any one group. Celebrities, as well as ordinary people, have fallen victim to the drug. Many musicians have admitted using heroin. The celebrity lifestyle lends itself to drug use. Celebrities often find themselves at wild parties with people offering them free drugs. They may also turn to drugs as a way to escape their busy lifestyles. Eric Clapton, Boy George, and Keith Richards of the Rolling Stones are all famous musicians who have admitted being addicted to heroin at one time. Sid Vicious of the Sex Pistols, Hillel Slovak of the Red Hot Chili Peppers, Jonathan Melvoin of Smashing Pumpkins, Shannon Hoon of Blind Melon, and Layne Staley of Alice in Chains all died from heroin-related causes. Kurt Cobain of Nirvana committed suicide by shooting himself, but at the time he had been

▲ *It seems that heroin use is particularly a problem among musicians and entertainers. Rock stars from many popular bands have died as a result of heroin use.*

STREET TERMS FOR HEROIN

Al Capone	Golden Girl	Ogoy
Antifreeze	Good horse	Old Steve
Ballot	H	Orange line
Bart Simpson	Hard candy	P-dope
Big bag	Hazel	Pangonadalot
Big H	Hero	Peg
Brown sugar	Hombre	Perfect high
Capital H	Horse	Poison
Cheese	HRN	Pure
China White	Isda	Rawhide
Chip	Jee gee	Ready rock
Crank	Jive	Salt
Dead on arrival	Joy	Shag
Dirt	Junk	Skag
Dope	Lemonade	Sweet dreams
Dr. Feelgood	Mexican brown	Train
Ferry dust	Nice and easy	White boy
George smack	Noise	Zoquete

Source: Office of National Drug Control Policy

heavily dosed with heroin. Jerry Garcia, guitar player for the Grateful Dead, died in his sleep at a clinic where he was trying to get off the drug.

With many of these famous people using heroin, young people are getting mixed messages. Celebrities have a big influence over the public. Many young people feel that heroin use must be helping the careers of these musicians by making them become more creative. In truth, it destroys talent and breaks up some of the most amazing bands. Legendary jazz singer Billie Holiday said, "If you think dope is for kicks and for thrills, you're out of your mind. . . . If you think you need stuff to play music or sing, you're crazy. It can fix you so you can't play nothing or sing nothing."[2]

Heroin Chic

In the 1990s, looking as though you were on heroin even became fashionable. "Heroin Chic" was an image often seen in television and magazine advertisements. Heroin chic models are extremely thin, and they walk around with a blank expression on their face. They have dark circles under their eyes and greasy hair. Fashion designers and advertisers made the look seem glamorous. David Sorrenti was a fashion photographer who promoted this look. He died at the age of twenty from a heroin overdose. In 1997, then-President Bill Clinton addressed the Heroin Chic look saying, ". . . heroin is not creative. It's destructive. It's not beautiful. It is ugly. And this is not about art. It's about life and death. And glorifying death is not good for any society."[3]

Recent Trends

In 2001, a U.S. Department of Health and Human Services National Household Survey found that about 3.1 million Americans had tried heroin at least once. It is hard to count the actual number of hard-core heroin users in the United States. However, it is estimated that there are between 750,000 and 1,000,000 people who are addicted to heroin.[4]

Chapter 3

EFFECTS OF HEROIN

Heroin usually comes in the form of a white or brown powder. It can be injected, smoked, or sniffed. If heroin is injected into the veins, the user will feel the results within seven to eight seconds. Most users inject the drug into their veins, while others inject it into their muscles. If the heroin is injected into muscle, or directly under the skin, it takes from five to eight minutes for

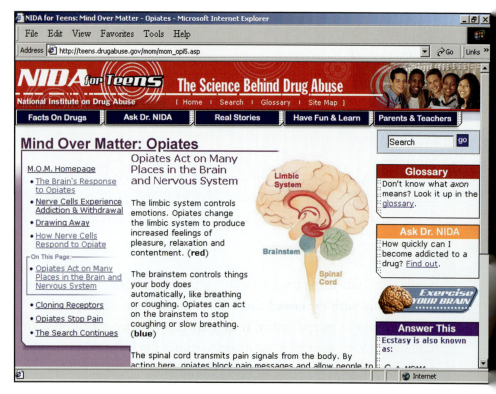

▲ Opiates, such as heroin, affect your brain in several ways. While producing relaxing and pleasurable feelings through your limbic system, opiates can also slow breathing. Also, opiates can block pain by affecting the spinal cord.

the drug to take effect. This is called skin popping. The faster the heroin gets to the brain, the quicker and more intense the effects. If the heroin is sniffed or snorted, the drug must be absorbed into the mucous membrane. The reaction takes from three to five minutes. As heroin has become purer, more and more users are sniffing it. This has led more young people to try the drug. For young people, sniffing heroin seems easier than injecting it. If it is smoked, the heroin enters the circulatory system through the lungs. Blood vessels then carry the drug through the bloodstream. It then takes the drug seven to ten seconds to enter the brain. Some addicts have been known to use the drug as many as four times a day.

When users inject heroin, they will feel a rush go through their bodies. They have a feeling of euphoria, or well-being. They will start to relax. Their skin may become flushed, and their mouth may feel dry. They will then nod off into a sleepy state. They will continue to nod in and out of sleep for a while as the drug travels through their bodies. It will become harder for users to do anything.

The first time a user injects the heroin, he or she will often feel sick to the stomach. This is because the body is not used to having heroin coursing through it. For some, this initial feeling is enough to stop taking heroin. Many, however, will try the drug again. Some users describe it as "pleasantly sick."

▶ Why People Use Heroin

People may start using heroin for different reasons. Some people want to fit in with the crowd and be like their friends. Some people take drugs to escape reality. If they are experiencing a painful time in their life, they may use drugs to numb the pain, whether it be physical or emotional. In reality, drugs will end up causing more pain to the user and the people that care for her or him. Some people take drugs because they falsely believe that it will make them more creative or make their problems disappear.

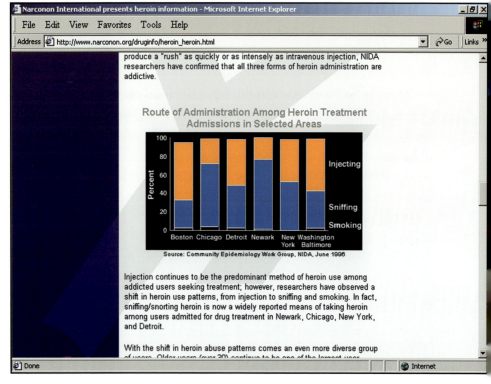

▲ Research has found that injecting heroin is the most common method of introducing the drug into a user's system. However, sniffing and smoking heroin are increasingly becoming more popular ways to take the drug.

Some think that they can try the drug once to see what it is like and then stop. This is almost always impossible. Heroin is highly physically addictive. Once someone starts taking the drug, it is likely he or she will continue to use it. The body starts to depend on the drug, and people continue to use it just so they do not get sick from withdrawal symptoms.

▶ A Deadly Mixture

Opium is brought to a heroin laboratory and converted to morphine. The morphine is then made into heroin. These heroin labs are mostly located in the countries that produce heroin. The heroin is then shipped to places such as the United States. In the United States, the drug dealer cuts the heroin. This means he or she adds other substances so that the heroin is not as strong. Dealers do this because a dose of pure heroin is deadly.

There is no supervision in the lab, and so no one can be sure what else is in a dose of heroin or how pure it is. These additives can be anything, including milk, sugar, baking soda, and other white powders. Sometimes it is even mixed with laundry detergents, talc, starch, curry powder, and Ajax cleaner. The additives alone can cause clogged blood vessels or blockages to the lungs, liver, kidneys, and brain. Often the whiter the heroin, the more pure it is, and the more deadly it can be.

Health Risks

The word "heroin" comes from the Greek word heros, which means a person with strength or ability. It was named for this because people who take the drug often have delusions that they are in some way heroic. They think that they are more powerful than they really are. Another way heroin affects the mind is that people who use it become very paranoid. Parts of the brain cannot function when heroin is in the body. This affects judgment and rationality. People on heroin often make poor decisions and cannot think straight.

With continued heroin use, the body begins to wither away. Muscles shrink and the body has trouble digesting food. Making even the simplest decisions becomes almost impossible. Often, users do not realize how badly the drug is affecting them.

In the short term, heroin reduces pain and anxiety. In the long term, heroin kills. The more a person uses heroin, the more he or she needs it. The body gets used to the drug, so to get the same effects, the user must actually use more and more of the drug. This vicious cycle causes the body to break down. Eventually a heroin user may have difficulty breathing. The user's body may also have a hard time fighting off diseases. Tooth decay, swollen gums, vomiting, constipation, poor eyesight, cold sweats, and itching are only some of the effects that can happen to a person addicted to heroin.

Sharing needles is another way many heroin users get sick. HIV, the virus that causes AIDS, can be passed from one person to another this way. Hepatitis, a disease that damages the liver, can also be passed on this way. Users risk bacterial and viral infections, stroke, collapsed veins, and lung infections. An air bubble in a syringe can cause a vein to blow up, resulting in death because the air blocks blood from circulating through the veins.

Since addicts have no way of knowing how pure the heroin is, they have no way of knowing if their bodies can handle the dosage. Their bodies may shut down, and they may fall into a

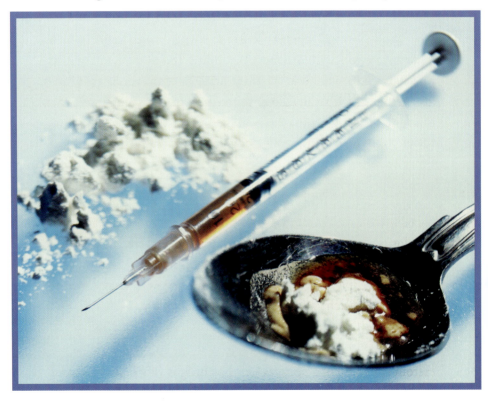

▲ Using a needle to inject heroin can be extremely dangerous. In addition to the dangers of the drug, users that share needles are at high risk of getting other diseases such as hepatitis or HIV, the virus that causes AIDS.

> Effects of Heroin

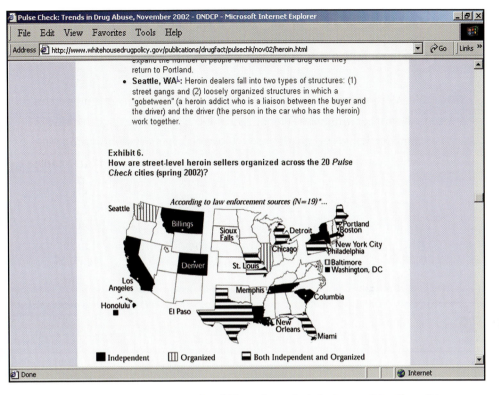

▲ In some cities, heroin is mainly sold by independent dealers, and in others it is sold by organized crime organizations, or both.

coma. This is called overdosing. Sometimes, people die from overdosing, as did Janis Joplin. If a user does survive an overdose, his or her brain may stop functioning correctly. In some rare instances, people have ended up paralyzed. A user may be confined to a wheelchair for the rest of his or her life.

▶ **Heroin and Lifestyle**

Heroin use changes a person's life. The drug is very expensive, and much of the time people turn to criminal activity such as stealing or prostitution to pay for it. Addicts may even start dealing the drug themselves to make money and have a ready supply.

Drug use also destroys trust. Friends and family often feel at a loss when they see a loved one ruining his or her life. An addict may begin to lie and steal to support his habit. Addicts often stop caring about their appearance and may even stop bathing. They have trouble keeping jobs and other commitments. When a person becomes addicted to heroin, everyone around him or her suffers. The only thing that really matters to addicts is where they are going to get their next fix. Phillip,* a nineteen-year-old former heroin addict, explains:

> From the day I started sniffing heroin, I stopped going to school on a regular basis. I had missed more than fifty days in a school year. At age sixteen, two years into my addiction, I started shooting up. I also started losing friends. I was manipulating people and doing pretty much whatever I had to so that I would feel better and not be in withdrawal. I was stealing from stores, family and friends, and I was going to risky areas to buy drugs. I overdosed at least five times.[1]

---

*While the stories of abuse in this book are real, many of the names have been changed.

Chapter 4 ▶

HOW HEROIN IS PRODUCED AND SOLD

To harvest heroin, the sap-like opium is taken from the poppy flower's pod. The opium is then taken to a lab where it is first processed into morphine and then further processed into heroin. Pure heroin is a fine, white powder. Sometimes it is gray or brown in color.

Although the primary sources of heroin are southern Asia, South America, and Mexico, the Middle East has been a large

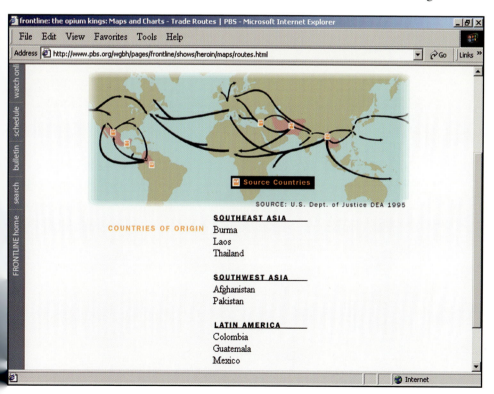

▲ Heroin is traded all over the world. However, it is produced primarily in southern Asia, South America, and Mexico.

source of the heroin trade during different times in history. Afghanistan, Iran, Turkey, and Pakistan are all countries known for producing the drug. It is produced for a small price and then sold for a much higher price in the United States. For example, in the year 2000, heroin that cost $2,720 to produce and sell in Pakistan was sold in the United States for $129,380.

Heroin trade has even provided money needed to fight wars. Terrorist groups in the Middle East have used money made from the drug trade to buy weapons and explosives. Colombian drug cartels are huge drug rings that smuggle drugs into the United States. Oftentimes, these drug cartels resemble well-armed militias. They are, in many cases, more powerful than the law enforcement agencies trying to stop them. In the United States, the Mafia, an organized crime group, also depends on money made from the illegal trading of drugs.

On the Street

Once heroin is in the United States, it is broken up into smaller bundles. Then it is sold to dealers on the street. The dealers further divide the heroin to sell to individuals for about twenty dollars for each bag. Dealers will sell to anyone, including schoolchildren. Once a person is addicted to heroin, the dealer's job is easy. People will search the dealer out and beg for more. William Burroughs wrote, "Junk is the ideal product . . . the ultimate merchandise. No sales talk is necessary. The client will crawl through a sewer and beg to buy."[1]

Drug Laws

In the early-twentieth century, there was a growing heroin problem in the United States. The crime rate due to drug use began to rise. The government stepped in and began to pass laws that would make both using drugs and dealing drugs a punishable crime. At first, drug laws were very strict. If someone sold drugs to a minor, he or she could be sentenced to death. Eventually

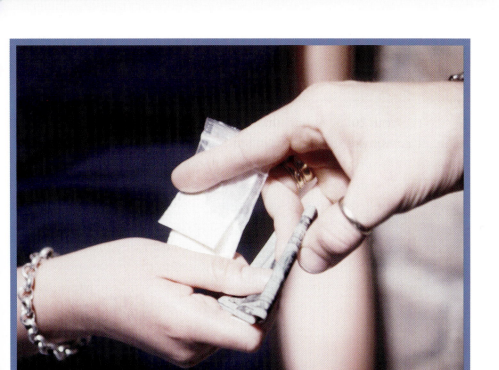

▲ *On the streets, heroin is usually sold in small bundles like the drugs exchanging hands here.*

these sentences were reduced. During the 1960s, efforts were made to help addicts stop using heroin and get back to a normal, healthy lifestyle, rather than convicting them of a crime and throwing them in jail. The Bureau of Drug Abuse Control and the Bureau of Narcotics and Dangerous Drugs were put into place to help solve the drug problem.

In 1970, the Controlled Substances Act, part of the Comprehensive Drug Abuse Prevention and Control Act, was passed. These acts separated drugs into different categories based on how dangerous they were to the public. The more dangerous the drug, the steeper the penalty for selling or possessing it. The

▲ Heroin is listed as a Schedule 1 drug by the United States' Controlled Substances Act. That means that if a person is caught with it, the stiffest penalties apply.

act further set up strict regulations for drug use and put penalties in place.

In 1971, President Nixon launched the War on Drugs campaign. He gave a speech saying that the United States had more heroin users than any other nation. He declared the drug problem a national emergency. In 1973, the Drug Enforcement Administration (DEA) was created. The people working for this group made sure federal drug laws were enforced. The DEA's officers work both in the United States and overseas to try to make sure drug trafficking is stopped.

The penalties for drug possession and drug dealing vary from state to state. The first offense for possession can include as much as a year in prison and a hefty fine. For each offense, the penalty becomes more severe. The penalty often depends on how much heroin a person has in his or her possession when caught. If a person is caught dealing drugs to a minor, the penalties are more severe. Depending on the amount of heroin involved, the person can get a sentencing that could possibly put him or her behind bars for the rest of his or her life.

Even with all of these laws in place, the drug problem in the United States has not stopped. Heroin has become more affordable, and more people from different income levels are turning to heroin use. The War on Drugs is an ongoing battle.

Chapter 5

RECOVERY

In 1994, there were just over sixty-three thousand heroin-related trips to hospital emergency rooms in the United States. By 2000, that number increased to over ninety-four thousand.[1] This is partly because a lot of the heroin on the street is purer than in the past. More people are sniffing heroin rather than shooting up. They may think this is a safer way to do the drug, and so they may even do more of it. This type of thinking has caused many more heroin-related deaths.

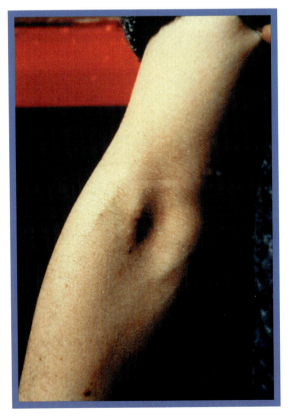

Heroin addiction happens when the user's brain gets used to the drug and depends on it to feel good. Many users realize that heroin is bad for them but continue to use it anyway. If the user tries to stop using the drugs, withdrawal symptoms occur. As the user continues to use more heroin, his or her body needs more and

◀ This image shows the damage that heroin use can do to a person's arm if it is frequently injected.

▶ 38 ◀

more of the drug to get the same feeling the next time he or she does it. This is because his body is developing a tolerance to the drug. Heroin withdrawal can be very uncomfortable for the user because the body has gotten so used to the drug. Some users continue to use heroin simply to avoid the discomfort of withdrawal.

▷ Withdrawal

About four to six hours after heroin is used, if no more is taken, the user will begin to feel the effects of withdrawal. His eyes will start to tear up, and he will experience flu-like symptoms, including sneezing, depression, weakness, cramping, vomiting, and diarrhea. Within the next two or three days, the symptoms will continue to get worse. Withdrawal is a horrible feeling. An addict going through heroin withdrawal cannot eat, sleep, and move around too much. This is because the body is trying to rebalance itself. It can take a week to ten days for the symptoms to disappear. Even first-time users feel the effects of withdrawal. This is one reason why heroin is so addictive. To prevent withdrawal symptoms, the user continues to take heroin.

The term "quitting cold turkey" comes from the idea that goose bumps sometimes appear over the body and make the user look like a plucked turkey. When someone quits cold turkey, he or she is stopping the drug use all at once, instead of doing it slowly. Muscle spasms may also occur, causing the legs to involuntarily kick. This is where the term "kicking the habit" comes from.

▷ Rehabilitation

The first step on the road to recovery from heroin addiction is admitting that there is a problem. A person on drugs must want to help herself. If she does not care about herself, then no amount of support will help her. An addict who wants to stop drug use must actively participate in a clean and sober lifestyle.

There are many different kinds of programs and rehabilitation centers that are dedicated to helping people addicted to

MyReportLinks.com Books

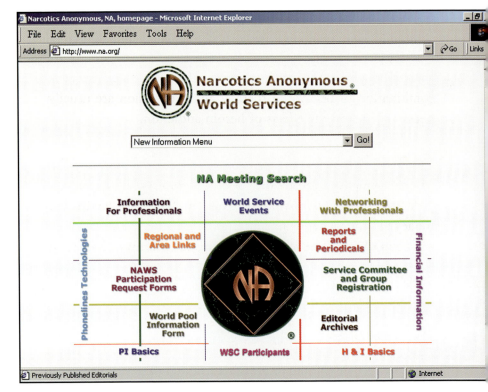

▲ Narcotics Anonymous is a nonprofit group for those who are addicted to drugs. The organization's weekly meetings are held to provide support for those trying to get or stay clean.

drugs. People who choose residential programs live in a facility for three to six months. During this time, they undergo treatment that will help them understand their drug problem and will put them back on track to a normal, healthy life. Outpatient therapy is similar except that the person does not live in a facility.

Along with therapy to help understand the problem and to change the behavior that led to drug addiction, people also take a drug called methadone. Being given methadone allows a heroin addict to function normally and reduces the craving for heroin. The drawback is that methadone itself can become addicting. In some cases, a former heroin junkie must receive methadone treatments for the rest of his or her life to avoid craving heroin.

Methadone clinics have been set up all over the United States for this purpose. The drug buprenorphine is now being used in primary care doctor's offices to treat opiate addiction. Naloxone and naltrexone are other drugs that block heroin addiction. A combination of behavioral therapy and medication are usually necessary to stop the effects of heroin addiction.

▶ **A Long Road**

Ms. Rodriguez is a former drug user with four children. She not only used drugs, but she also began to deal so she could make money to support her own habit. At the time this was written, she was going through the rehabilitation process. She says, "I focus on

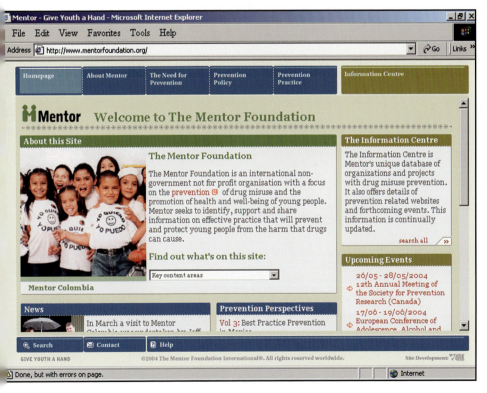

▲ The Mentor Foundation seeks to prevent drug misuse among youth, and instead, promote a healthy lifestyle. This international nonprofit group conducts its own global research and works with governments to develop effective drug policies.

MyReportLinks.com Books

▲ Heroin is a deadly habit that is difficult to recover from. If you know someone who is using heroin, try to find a way to get him or her help immediately.

my children, on staying clean and hopefully totally being human again."[2] Ms. Rodriguez hit rock bottom before she was able to find a way to get her life back together. Her children watched as she did drugs and began to destroy her life. Today her life is better because she got the help she needed.

Heroin addicts need a lot of support as they go through the recovery process. That is why there are programs not only for the addicts themselves, but for their family members as well. This allows addicts to see how their drug problem has affected the ones they love. It also allows family members to actively participate in the recovery process. It is important for families to learn the factors that caused a loved one to use or to return to using heroin. They must be supportive of the recovery process. They must also learn to deal with family issues that may have contributed to the drug use. Families should discuss problems and keep the lines of communication open.

People in recovery programs have many different ways of dealing with their addiction. One important way is to talk with their counselor about their fears. They may also choose to keep a journal and write down their feelings. After the first few months, recovering addicts are encouraged to continue to go to recovery meetings, possibly for the rest of their lives. This allows them to talk with people who have gone through similar experiences. It also provides them with the support they need.

Former addicts must also learn new ways to deal with stressful situations in their lives. For example, they may get involved with exercise programs or meditation. This will ensure that they have an outlet other than drugs.

Approaching an Adult for Help

If you or someone you know has a drug problem, it is important to talk with an adult you trust. This can be a parent, teacher, principal, or anyone else in your community who you think may be able to help you. Do not be afraid to tell them that you or your

NUMBER OF EMERGENCY DEPARTMENT MENTIONS OF HEROIN

YEAR	EMERGENCY ROOM VISITS
1994	63,158
1995	69,556
1996	72,980
1997	70,712
1998	75,688
1999	82,192
2000	94,804
2001	93,064
2002	93,519

*Source: Drug Abuse Warning Network

friend needs help. If your parent has a drug problem and you would like to get him or her help, it is also a good idea to approach an adult you can trust.

There are many programs that help family members deal with a loved one's drug abuse. You can contact a number of organizations to ask questions about where there might be a drug treatment center near your home or how to get yourself, a friend, or a family member into treatment. One of these organizations is the Center for Substance Abuse Treatment (CSAT). CSAT is a toll-free, twenty-four-hour treatment referral service to help you find counseling and treatment options locally. Two other good organizations to contact are Covenant House and Narcotics Anonymous. Look in your local phone book or search online to find the phone number for the organization in your area.

Glossary

addiction—The uncontrollable need to use or abuse a drug such as heroin.

buprenorphine—A drug used to treat opiate addiction that works like methadone but according to some doctors, has less side effects.

codeine—A morphine derivative made from the poppy plant. Codeine is a drug that is mainly prescribed by doctors as a pain killer or as a cough suppressant.

drug trafficking—The shipment, sale, and trade of illegal narcotics.

euphoria—A feeling of extreme happiness and contentment.

methadone clinic—A rehabilitation facility where patients are prescribed methadone, a narcotic that doctors use to help treat heroin addiction.

morphine—A narcotic that is sometimes used as a painkiller.

mucous membrane—A thin layer that contains mucous glands and protects the interior of the body from outside pollutants. Mucous membranes line the throat, mouth, lungs, eyelids, and other areas.

naloxone and naltrexone—Drugs used in treatment of heroin addiction. Naloxone blocks a drug from affecting the nervous system.

opiates—Drugs (such as morphine or codeine) that contain or are made from opium and tend to induce sleep and alleviate pain.

opium dens—A secret place with usually poor conditions where users would go to use opium.

overdose—To take a deadly or toxic amount of a drug.

skin popping—Injecting a drug under the skin but not into a vein.

thebaine—An opiate that is used to create other medicines such as naloxone, naltrexone, and buprenorphine.

Chapter Notes

Chapter 1. Wasted Talent
1. Myra Friedman, *Buried Alive: The Biography of Janis Joplin* (New York: Crown Publishing Group, 1999), p. 158.
2. Ibid., p. 319.

Chapter 2. The History of Heroin
1. Martin Booth, *Opium: A History* (New York: St. Martin's Griffin, 1999), p. 205.
2. Billie Holiday with William Dufty, *Lady Sings the Blues,* 1956, as reprinted in *The Columbia World of Quotations,* 1996, <http://www.bartleby.com/66/14/28714.html> (March 25, 2004).
3. President Bill Clinton, "Remarks by the President at U.S. Conference of Mayors," *White House Press Release,* May 21, 1997, <http://www.treatment.org/news/mayors.html> (March 25, 2004).
4. Jennifer Lloyd, "Heroin: June 2003," *Drug Policy Information Clearinghouse,* June 2003, <http://www.whitehousedrugpolicy.gov/publications/factsht/heroin/index.html> (April 19, 2004).

Chapter 3. Effects of Heroin
1. Caucus on International Narcotics Control, "Phillip: Heroin Survivor," *The Domestic Consequences of Heroin Use,* May 9, 2000, <http://www.drugcaucus.senate.gov/heroinphillip.html> (April 19, 2004).

Chapter 4. How Heroin Is Produced and Sold
1. William Burroughs, *The Naked Lunch,* 1959, as reprinted in *The Columbia World of Quotations,* 1996, <www.bartleby.com/66/59/9359.html> (March 25, 2004).

Chapter 5. Recovery
1. Jennifer Lloyd, "Heroin," *ONDCP Drug Policy Information Clearinghouse Fact Sheet,* June 2003, <http://www.whitehousedrugpolicy.gov/publications/factsht/heroin/> (May 26, 2004).
2. Christine Hauser, "A Mother's Battle to Break a Vicious Cycle of Addiction," *New York Times,* November 16, 2003, p. 41.

Further Reading

Cobb, Allan. *Heroin and Your Veins: The Incredibly Disgusting Story.* New York: Rosen Publishing Group, Inc., 2000.

Cothran, Helen. *Heroin.* Farmington Hills, Mich.: Gale Group, 2001.

Howard, Todd. *Heroin.* San Diego, Calif.: Lucent Books, 2003.

Hyde, Margaret O., and John F. Setaro. *Drugs 101: An Overview for Teens.* Brookfield, Conn.: Twenty First Century Books, 2003.

Kerrigan, Michael. *The War Against Drugs.* Broomall, Pa.: Mason Crest Publishers, 2003.

Littell, Mary Ann. *Heroin Drug Dangers.* Berkeley Heights, N.J.: Enslow Publishers, Inc., 2000.

Sonder, Ben. *All About Heroin.* Danbury, Conn.: Scholastic Library Publishing, 2002.

Westcott, Patsy. *Why Do People Take Drugs?* Austin, Tex.: Raintree Steck-Vaughn Publishers, 2001.

Woods, Geraldine. *Heroin.* Berkeley Heights, N.J.: Enslow Publishers, Inc., 2001.

Numbers to Call for Help

Center for Substance Abuse Treatment National Hotline
 1-800-662-4357

Covenant House
 1-800-999-9999

NAADAC, The Association for Addiction Professionals
 1-800-548-0497

Narcotics Anonymous
 1-818-773-9999

National Helplines
 1-800-HELP-111

Index

A
addiction, 14, 38–41
additives, 29
Alice in Chains, 24
B
Bayer pharmaceutical company, 20
Beat Generation, 22
Big Brother and the Holding Company, 12
Blind Melon, 24
Boy George, 24
buprenorphine, 41
Bureau of Drug Abuse Control, 35
Bureau of Narcotics and Dangerous Drugs, 35
Burroughs, William, 22, 34
C
celebrities, 23–24
Center for Substance Abuse Treatment (CSAT), 44
Clapton, Eric, 24
Clinton, Bill, 24
Cobain, Kurt, 24
codeine, 17, 20
Comprehensive Drug Abuse Prevention and Control Act, 25
Controlled Substances Act, 35–36
Covenant House, 44
D
Dreser, Heinrich, 20
Drug Enforcement Administration, 37
E
effects, 26–27, 29–31
G
Garcia, Jerry, 24
Grateful Dead, The, 24
H
Heroin Act of 1924, 22
heroin chic, 24
heroin laboratory, 28–29
HIV, 30
Holiday, Billie, 24
Hoon, Shannon, 24
J
Joplin, Janis, 10–15, 31

K
Kerouac, Jack, 22
M
Mafia, 24
Melvoin, Jonathan, 24
methadone, 40–41
morphine, 17, 20, 28
N
naloxone, 41
naltrexone, 41
Narcotics Anonymous, 44
Nirvana, 24
Nixon, Richard, 35
O
opium, 12, 16–21, 28, 33
opium dens, 17
Opium War, 17–20
P
poppy plant, 12, 16–18, 33
Pure Food and Drug Act of 1906, 20
R
reasons, 27–28
Red Hot Chili Peppers, 24
rehabilitation, 39–41
Richards, Keith, 24
Rolling Stones, The, 24
S
Sex Pistols, The, 24
skin popping, 26–27
Slovak, Hillel, 24
Smashing Pumpkins, 24
Sorrenti, David, 24
sources, 16, 33–34
Staley, Layne, 24
street gangs, 21, 31
street names, 16
V
Vicious, Sid, 24
W
War on Drugs campaign, 35, 37
withdrawal, 28, 38–39
Woodstock festival (1969), 14
Wright, C. R. Alder, 20
Z
Zexu, Lin, 17–19